Perking Up Poe

Brian Eltz

ISBN 978-1-0980-7754-9 (paperback)
ISBN 978-1-63903-427-7 (hardcover)
ISBN 978-1-0980-7756-3 (digital)

Christian Faith Publishing, Inc.
832 Park Avenue
Meadville, PA 16335
www.christianfaithpublishing.com

Printed in the United States of America

For my wife,
the greatest cause of all my smiles.

I felt that I breathed an atmosphere of sorrow.

—From "The Fall of the House of Usher"

Blessed are the sorrowing,
for they shall be comforted.

—Matthew 5:4

Once upon an afternoon, outside there was rain and gloom.

Mother sent us up to see the boarder in room 204.

Mr. Poe had seemed too sad in recent days, so far from glad.

In truth, it made us all feel bad, so we would make him smile, and more!

"You knock," Maddy said to me, "and I will hide behind the door.

This will cheer him up for sure."

"Ahhhhh!" distinctly he did shout, when my masked sister jumped out.
I then rushed to pick the startled Mr. Poe from off the floor.

"Sorry, Edgar! My twin sis thought that her joke just couldn't miss."

"Roddy, don't apologize. I bet that made his spirit soar!"

"Actually, young Miss Usher, my heart has skipped a beat or more.
Mind the cat and shut the door."

"December always gets me down," he said and tried to hide his frown.

"I do appreciate you tried to cheer me up, but please no more."

I turned and winked at my fair twin. She nodded, then said, "Let's begin.

We'll get you to display a grin by dinnertime—maybe before.

And if you haven't smiled by then, tomorrow we'll have more in store."

That idea shook him to his core.

Maddy, being far from meek, was first to shout out, "Hide-and-seek!"

We will hide, and Mr. Edgar, you must count: 1, 2, 3, 4…

And so on, till you get to 10, and you will come and find us then."

He said, "Go hide then if you can. I'd bet my head I'll find you, for

My room is small. Where will you hide? Within the wall? Beneath the floor?"

That made us have to think some more.

"You may be right," I said, agreeing. "Let's play a game with less competing."

I looked around, and then I found the thing I had been looking for.

"We'll take this deck of cards and build a structure till the table's filled."

Edgar's look was less than thrilled, but still we started the ground floor.

"Build it high, and *higher*!" I said. "We'll keep on adding more, and *more*!"

Maddy said, "It will fall, for sure."

My house of Usher grew and grew, but Mr. Edgar's frown did too.

"Thank you, Roddy. Thank you, Maddy. But my mood is still quite poor."

Just then came a sudden knocking. With surprise it sent us rocking.

The house *didn't* fall (and that was shocking). Another knock came at the door.

Mr. Edgar rose and walked across his room to get the door.

He opened it—to Mr. Moore.

"Good afternoon," said Mr. Moore, the morning postman at the door.

"I brought this note and package up, instead of down with Mrs. U—.
I had this parcel with no name this morning, when at first I came,
Then found the note had somehow lain apart from it, but it's for you.
I'd feared the letter'd been purloined, but here it is. My route is through.
Let me bring the crate in too."

Saying bye to Mr. M—, we analyzed the box, and then
Mr. Edgar pulled his chair in front of box, and us, and door.
It was from his friend Annie, who said that she and her husband knew
This time of year could make him blue, and so to cheer his spirit more,
She'd sent an early birthday gift to ease the burdens that he bore.
"This gift will make you smile," she swore.

Mr. Edgar's cat didn't smile, sniffing 'round the box a while,

Mewing angrily, when we then heard the box make noise itself.

"Dear Annie's given me strange gifts over the years. Some things like this:

An odd Gold Bug (The cat went *hiss*)…that can of worms there on the shelf.

I know no one who'd use such bait, and I'm no fisherman myself,

So it just rests there on my shelf."

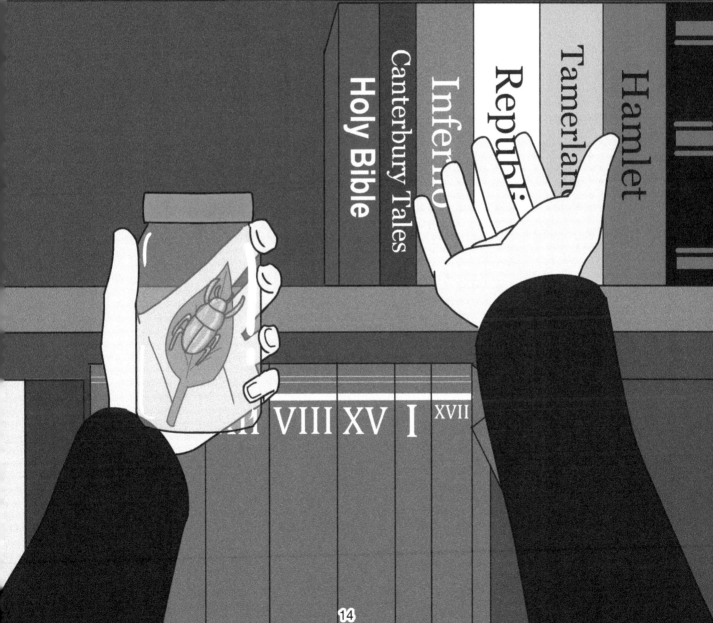

Maddy dared him to unseal it. He hesitated, then revealed it,

Opening up the box, there came a stately bird—large, black, and strong.

"A raven?!" Mr. Poe was yelling, as his cat set to propelling

Herself up to the light, no telling if it could hold her weight for long

Or if the furry pendulum would snag the bird before too long.

Together these two did *not* belong!

ELDORADO SHIPPING Co.

IN SUNSHINE AND IN SHADOW

The cat and light then fell down crashing, while the raven circled, thrashing,

My card house of Usher smashing—scattered all around the room.

I tried to rein Poe's mad cat in, while Maddy sat there with a grin.

Poor Edgar! Seems he just couldn't win. He sat quietly, full of gloom.

Suddenly the shadowed raven perched upon his head to groom—

Perched, and spread his wings to groom.

Maddy held Poe's cat, while I sat wondering if he'd scream or cry,
    But for some cause (I don't know why) he did something ne'er seen before.
Slow at first, his silent stare, took in all that had happened there,
    His stiffened face grew soft and fair as he let out a joyous roar.
    He could not help but laugh and smile as we all sat upon the floor,
                    Laughing at the "hat" he wore.

"Maddy, Roddy—I must say, this has been quite a shocking day.
    It started off quite somber but has come to a most curious end.
It looks as if eight apes uncaged had stormed my room with all their rage,
    But your advice has been quite sage, and now I have this wingéd friend,
    To add to you two, and sweet Annie, and my cat—friend upon friend.
                    I'll have a *thank you* note to send."

And that raven, never flitting, still was sitting…still was sitting
  On dear Edgar's head as he began to straighten up the room.
And we thought that we might aid him, except then our mother came in,
  So shocked that she nearly fainted—her face whiter than a tomb.
  She had come to tell us dinner was set out in the front room.
    Quoth Mr. Poe: "I'll be down soon."

Also by Brian Eltz:

Shaking Up Shakespeare

About the Author

Brian Eltz is originally from Carbondale, Pennsylvania, and earned his BA and MA in English literature from The University of Scranton. After moving to Lancaster, Pennsylvania, he began teaching English composition at Harrisburg Area Community College, where he has been an adjunct professor for over ten years. Brian is also a stay-at-home dad. He lives in Millersville, Pennsylvania, with his wife, three young sons, and a cat.